ASTRID & APOLLO

AND THE
FISHING FLOP

BY
V.T. BIDANIA

ILLUSTRATED BY
DARA LASHIA LEE

PICTURE WINDOW BOOKS
a capstone imprint

To Mahal, who took me fishing. — V.T.B.

Astrid and Apollo is published by Picture Window Books,
an imprint of Capstone.
1710 Roe Crest Drive
North Mankato, Minnesota 56003
www.capstonepub.com

Library of Congress Cataloging-in-Publication Data
Names: Bidania, V. T., author. | Lee, Dara Lashia, illustrator.
Title: Astrid and Apollo and the fishing flop / by V.T. Bidania ;
    illustrated by Dara Lashia Lee.
Description: North Mankato, Minnesota : Picture Window Books, an imprint of
    Capstone, [2020] | Series: Astrid and Apollo | Audience: Ages 6-8. |
    Summary: Hmong-American twins Astrid and Apollo are on their very first
    fishing trip, but while Astrid catches three fine fish, Apollo's line
    keeps snagging on non-fish things, and when a summer storm brings the
    trip to a sudden end Apollo admits he is disappointed with the
    experience—until he gets a look at the funny pictures their dad has
    taken.
Identifiers: LCCN 2019058187 (print) | LCCN 2019058188 (ebook) | ISBN
    9781515861232 (hardcover) | ISBN 9781515861270 (paperback) | ISBN
    9781515861287 (adobe pdf)
Subjects: LCSH: Hmong American children—Juvenile fiction. | Hmong American
    families—Juvenile fiction. | Twins—Juvenile fiction. | Brothers and
    sisters—Juvenile fiction. | Fishing stories. | CYAC: Hmong
    Americans—Fiction. | Twins—Fiction. | Brothers and sisters—Fiction. |
    Fishing—Fiction.
Classification: LCC PZ7.1.B5333 An 2020 (print) | LCC PZ7.1.B5333 (ebook)
    | DDC [Fic]—dc23
LC record available at https://lccn.loc.gov/201905818
LC ebook record available at https://lccn.loc.gov/2019058188

Designer: Lori Bye

Design Elements: Shutterstock: Ingo Menhard, Yangxiong

Table of Contents

ASTRID GAO NOU

Hi, I'm Astrid. My twin brother is Apollo, and we were born in Minnesota. We live here with our mom, dad, and little sister, Eliana.

Hi, I'm Apollo! Our mom and dad were both born in Laos. They came to the United States when they were very young and grew up here.

APOLLO NOU KOU

MOM, DAD, AND ELIANA GAO CHEE

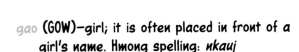

gao (GOW)—girl; it is often placed in front of a girl's name. Hmong spelling: *nkauj*

Gao Chee (GOW chee)—shiny girl. Hmong spelling: *Nkauj Ci*

Gao Nou (GOW new)—sun girl. Hmong spelling: *Nkauj Hnub*

Hmong (MONG)—a group of people who came to the U.S. from Laos. Many Hmong from Laos now live in Minnesota. Hmong spelling: *Hmoob*

Nou Kou (NEW koo)—star. Hmong spelling: *Hnub Qub*

tou (TOO)—boy or son; it is often placed in front of a boy's name. Hmong spelling: *tub*

Tickle Box

"Over here! Kick it this way!" said Apollo.

Astrid kicked the soccer ball toward him, but it missed Apollo. The ball bounced on the ground and rolled into the garage.

"I'll get it!" said Apollo.

The sun shined on his face as he chased the ball.

The wind blew at the trees, shaking the branches. It was a warm and windy day.

As Apollo ran after the ball, he didn't see the thin white wire on the garage floor. His shoe got stuck in the wire. Apollo tripped and fell down.

"Hey!" he said.

Astrid came running. "What happened?" she asked. "Are you okay?"

Apollo sat up. The wire was wrapped around his ankle.

"What's that?" said Astrid.

Dad hurried over from where he was cleaning the car.

"Are you all right?" he said.

Apollo nodded.

Astrid showed the wire to Dad. "This tripped him!"

"You found my line," said Dad. He helped Apollo unwrap the line and pulled him up. "I'm sorry. That fell out of the car."

"What's it for?" said Apollo.

"I'll show you," Dad said.

Astrid and Apollo followed him to the back of the car.

Dad held up the line. "Twins, take a good look."

They looked closer at the line. Then they looked inside the car trunk. They saw a plastic box with a handle. It looked like a toolbox.

Astrid pointed at the box. "What's that called again? Is it a tickle box?"

Apollo suddenly remembered. "It's a tackle box!"

"Yes! Tomorrow I'm taking you fishing," said Dad.

"Thanks, Dad!" Astrid said happily.

"We've wanted to go fishing for so long!" said Apollo.

Dad smiled. "Remember? We had to wait for fishing season to open. It starts tomorrow. The weather should be perfect."

"We can use the fishing poles we got for Christmas," said Astrid.

"Finally!" said Apollo.

Mom and Dad had given them fishing poles for Christmas. Astrid got a shiny green pole. Apollo got a bright blue pole.

"Get to bed on time tonight. We're leaving early in the morning," Dad said.

"Now we can learn how to fish! We can take pictures holding a fish too," said Apollo.

Dad nodded. "Yes!"

Apollo had seen pictures of his cousins fishing. In each picture, they held up the big fish they caught. They smiled the happiest smiles.

Now it was his turn. Apollo couldn't wait to take pictures with all the big fish he would catch! He liked making people laugh. He would make sure to smile a happy smile. He would make sure his pictures were funny and silly.

Just then, the wind blew again. The fishing line fell to the ground. Astrid and Apollo chased the line down the sunny driveway.

* * *

Apollo was still sleeping when a light shined under his bedroom door. It woke him up. He turned to the clock by his bed. It was 5:00 in the morning!

The door opened. Dad was in the hallway. "Time to get up!"

Apollo hid his face under the pillow. "It's so early."

"We want to get to the lake before the sun rises. That's when the fish start biting. Did I tell you we get to ride in Uncle Lue's boat?" Dad said.

Apollo sat up. "Really?"

Uncle Lue had a big, fast boat he used for fishing every summer. Apollo and Astrid always wanted to ride in the boat, but they'd never had a chance.

"Yes," said Dad. "Now please wake up your sister. I'll go finish packing supplies."

Apollo hopped out of bed. He ran across the hall to Astrid's room. He knocked on the door and said, "Astrid?"

"Come in," she said sleepily.

Apollo pushed open the door. "Get up! Dad's taking us fishing now."

Astrid yawned. "Why so early?"

"We have to get there before sunrise. Dad said we get to ride in Uncle Lue's boat!"

Astrid's eyes opened wide. "His big, fast boat?"

"Yes!" said Apollo.

"Yay!" said Astrid.

Big and Juicy

When Apollo got to the kitchen, he smelled eggs and bacon. A pot of chicken in lemongrass was boiling next to the pan. Behind that, steam came out of the rice cooker.

Mom was by the stove. "Good morning," she said.

"Good morning! Where's Dad?" said Apollo.

Mom pointed to the side door with a big spoon. "He's in the garage."

"Thanks." Apollo smiled a big, happy smile. "Mom, I'll be smiling like this for pictures I take with the fish. They'll be the goofiest pictures in the world!"

"I can't wait to see them!" said Mom.

Apollo grabbed a piece of bacon, put on his shoes, and stepped into the garage.

Dad was putting life vests in the car.

Apollo saw the fishing poles on top of the car. "Dad, don't forget those!"

"Thanks! We can't fish without these." Dad set them in the car.

Mom and Astrid came out with bags of food.

"Here are bacon and egg sandwiches for breakfast, and boiled chicken and rice for lunch," said Mom.

"And coconut juice and jelly cups for fun," said Astrid.

"Thank you!" Dad said.

"What else do we need?" Apollo asked.

"There's one last thing we need, but we will pick it up with Uncle Lue. Now it's time to go!" said Dad.

The twins and Dad got into the car.

As Dad drove out of the garage, Astrid and Apollo looked out the car window. It was still dark outside.

Mom stood by the front door carrying Eliana.

Astrid opened the window. "Bye, Eliana."

"I'll take funny pictures for you," said Apollo.

Eliana kept her head on Mom's shoulder. She looked sad, like she wanted to go, but Mom said she was too young to fish all day.

"Have fun," Mom said. "Bring back some fish for dinner!"

"We will, Mom!" said Astrid.

"We'll bring back the biggest fish you ever saw!" said Apollo.

Mom smiled. "As long as you have fun, that's all that counts."

* * *

When they got to Uncle Lue's house, they saw his big truck parked in front. The boat was behind the truck, shining under the streetlight. It was even bigger than the truck.

Uncle Lue was wiping the side of
the boat.

"Hi, Uncle Lue!" Apollo said
when they got out of the car.

"Your boat looks so shiny!" said Astrid.

Uncle Lue laughed. "Hi, kids! You have to wipe it to keep the shine. Now who wants to go fishing?"

Dad and Uncle Lue packed the fishing supplies into the boat. They tied everything down. Astrid and Apollo climbed into the back seats of the truck. Dad and Uncle Lue sat in the front.

Apollo was looking forward to the boat ride. "How fast is your boat, Uncle Lue?" he asked.

"It's fast, but with kids on board, I promise not to go too fast," said Uncle Lue.

Apollo frowned at Astrid. She frowned back. They wanted to go fast.

Then Uncle Lue drove to a small store by the gas station. "I'll be right back!" he said.

When he came back, he said, "I got our bait."

Astrid looked at the container he was holding. "Are those worms?" she asked.

Apollo read the words *NIGHT CRAWLERS* on the container. "They are!" he said.

"Not just any worms. These are special. They're big and juicy," said Uncle Lue.

Apollo grinned.

"I don't want to touch them!" Astrid said.

Apollo didn't want to touch the worms either. But he wanted to catch fish. "I'll do it," he said.

Dad smiled. "They're not so bad. I'll show you how to put them on the fish hook."

Astrid shook her head. "No way!"

Dad, Apollo, and Uncle Lue laughed. Astrid couldn't help but laugh too.

As Uncle Lue drove out of the city, Astrid and Apollo ate the bacon and egg sandwiches. As they passed small towns, big farms, and huge parks, they drank coconut juice.

Finally, they reached a large lake.

The sun was rising. The sky turned a light blue color.

Dad pointed up ahead. "There it is, twins. That's where we'll be fishing."

Astrid and Apollo stared at the lake. It was so big. The water looked pretty under the sunrise.

"Time to launch the boat!" said Uncle Lue. He backed up the truck until the boat was in the water.

Dad unhooked the boat from the truck and tied it to the dock.

After Uncle Lue left to park the truck, Dad passed out life vests. "We need to always wear these when on the boat or dock," he said.

Suddenly the wind blew so hard, Astrid's hair flew in the air. It hit Apollo's face.

"It sure is windy this morning!" Dad said.

Then Uncle Lue came back and climbed into the boat. "Get in, kids!"

Dad helped Astrid and Apollo get into the boat before he hopped in. The boat wobbled in the water.

As everyone sat in their seats, Apollo looked out at the lake. "This is so cool!"

Dad untied the boat from the dock. Uncle Lue turned on the motor.

"All right, everybody. Let's go!" he said.

How Much Longer?

The boat zoomed forward. Water sprayed up the sides. Tiny drops fell on Astrid's and Apollo's arms.

"This is so fun!" Astrid laughed.

Apollo nodded. "It's really fun!"

"Hold on tight!" Uncle Lue steered the boat to the side. Astrid and Apollo held on to their seats as they leaned to the side.

The sun was up now. The boat moved along, faster and faster.

Waves rose up and down. The boat went right over the waves. The wind blew at their faces.

"I wish we could do this every day!" said Apollo.

"Me too!" said Astrid.

When they were close to the middle of the lake, Uncle Lue slowed down. The boat motor grew quiet.

"Now we can fish," Dad said.

He handed out the fishing poles and gave Astrid and Apollo each a pair of gloves.

"When you hold a fish," Dad said, "be sure to wear gloves to protect your hands. But first it's time for bait."

"Do I have to use a night crawler?" Astrid said.

"Would you rather use lures?" Uncle Lue opened the tackle box. Inside were plastic and rubber minnows in bright colors.

"Oh, those little fish are so cute. Yes, please!" Astrid said.

Uncle Lue helped Astrid hang a pink and green minnow on her hook. Dad helped Apollo put a night crawler on his hook.

Apollo made a face. "My bait is so mushy!"

"So is mine!" said Astrid.

"But mine is real and yours is fake!" Apollo said.

Astrid laughed.

Dad showed them the parts of
the pole. "This is the rod, this is the
reel, and this is the bobber. This is
how you cast." He swung the pole to
the side and tossed the fishing line
into the water.

Text copyright © 2021 by V.T. Bidania.
Illustrations copyright © 2021 by Capstone.